# AFRICAN-AMERICAN
# CHILDREN'S STORIES

## A TREASURY OF TRADITIONAL TALES

Cover illustrated by
Angela Jarecki

publications international, ltd.

Published by
Louis Weber, C.E.O., Publications International, Ltd.
7373 North Cicero Avenue, Lincolnwood, Illinois 60712

Ground Floor, 59 Gloucester Place, London W1U 8JJ

Customer Service: 1-800-595-8484 or customer_service@pilbooks.com

**www.pilbooks.com**

p i kids is a registered trademark of Publications International, Ltd.

8 7 6 5 4 3 2 1

ISBN-13: 978-1-4127-6091-1
ISBN-10: 1-4127-6091-7

# CONTENTS

SONG: THIS LITTLE LIGHT OF MINE  4

THE MAGIC BONES  5

SONG: DOWN IN MY HEART  14

THE DAUGHTER OF THE SUN AND THE MOON  15

SONG: GO TELL IT ON THE MOUNTAIN  24

GOOD BLANCHE, BAD ROSE, AND THE MAGIC EGGS  25

SONG: THIS TRAIN  34

TORTOISE, HARE, AND THE SWEET POTATOES  35

SONG: SWING LOW, SWEET CHARIOT  44

JOHN HENRY  45

MALAIKA AND BR'ER RABBIT  54

WHEN THE SAINTS GO MARCHIN' IN  62

WILEY AND THE HAIRY MAN  63

THE COMING OF NIGHT  72

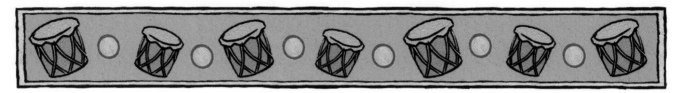

# THIS LITTLE LIGHT OF MINE

This little light of mine,
I'm gonna let it shine.
Oh, this little light of mine,
I'm gonna let it shine.

This little light of mine,
I'm gonna let it shine.
Let it shine,
Let it shine,
Let it shine.

This little light of mine,
I'm gonna let it shine.
Oh, this little light of mine,
I'm gonna let it shine.

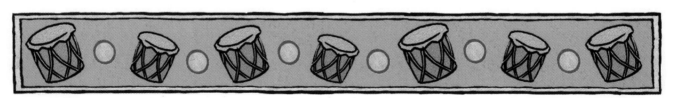

# THE MAGIC BONES

Adapted by Yon Walls
Illustrated by Leigh Toldi

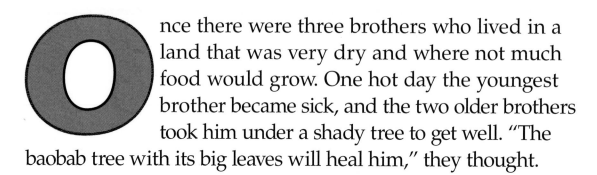

Once there were three brothers who lived in a land that was very dry and where not much food would grow. One hot day the youngest brother became sick, and the two older brothers took him under a shady tree to get well. "The baobab tree with its big leaves will heal him," they thought.

After three days and three nights the youngest brother still did not feel better. The older brothers left the sick brother all by himself. The sick brother cried, "Please don't leave me!" But they left him anyway.

One day, the youngest brother began to feel better. He made his home under the baobab tree and built a big box with branches and thorns to catch food.

He put the box near a village. When he returned the next day to see if he had caught food for dinner, he saw that an old man was trapped in the box.

"I know you are hungry," said the old man. "I have some magic bones. Throw the bones and make a wish."

The boy threw the magic bones, and suddenly cassava plants appeared. As the boy ate the tasty cassava, the old man said, "I will soon die. My name is Jambajimbira, which means 'jumping drum.' When I die, I will leave the magic bones to you. Just take the bones to a grassy field, throw them, and say my name. After you throw them you will get whatever you want." Then the old man died.

The boy found a grassy field, threw the magic bones, and called out Jambajimbira's name. Then the boy said, "Let there be a large village and plenty of food." Right before his eyes appeared a large village full of people, and there was lots of food for everyone. The villagers called the boy "Jambajimbira."

The two brothers who had left their youngest brother under the shady baobab tree heard about the chief named Jambajimbira. They traveled to his village to speak to him. "Jambajimbira, we are hungry!" they said. Jambajimbira gave each of them a bowl of milk and asked them to drink.

"Have you forgotten me?" Jambajimbira said to the two brothers. "I am your youngest brother!"

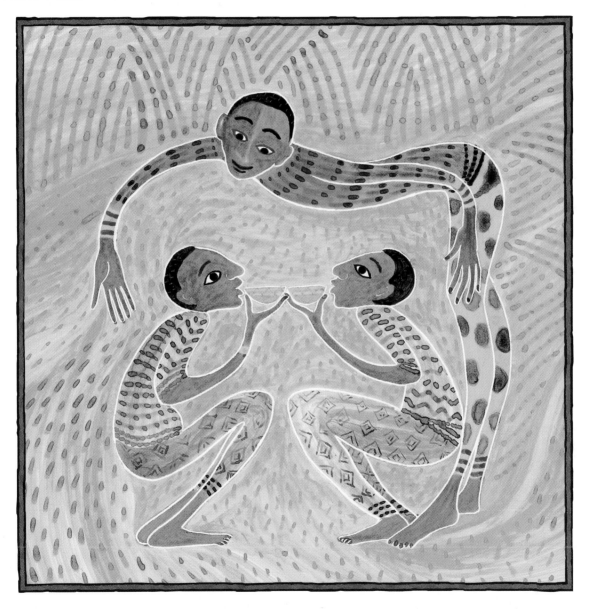

When the brothers heard Jambajimbira speak they began to cry. "Oh brother, we missed you!" they said.

Jambajimbira forgave them and said, "You can live in my village, and I will give each of you wives."

After months of living in the village, the two brothers wanted to be like Jambajimbira and rule a village. "We are the older brothers," they thought. "We should rule a fine village. If we can find the magic bones we can become chiefs."

While Jambajimbira was away from the village, the two brothers found the magic bones and wished for a village all their own. They also made their brother's village disappear.

When Jambajimbira returned and found out what his brothers had done, he started to cry. Kalib the rat and Ngabi the great hawk saw this and said, "Jambajimbira, stop crying. We will help you get back the magic bones. But what will you give us in return?"

"Anything you wish," replied Jambajimbira.

Kalib said, "I want lots of nuts," and Ngabi said, "I want chickens."

The rat ran and the hawk flew to the village of the two brothers. Kalib crawled into the largest house in the village and quietly dragged out the bones. One of the villagers saw him and shouted, "The chiefs' magic bones are being carried away by the rat!" Then Ngabi swooped down and flew away with Kalib. The villagers shouted, "Well done!" They believed the hawk would eat the rat.

But Ngabi carried Kalib and the magic bones back to Jambajimbira, who was filled with joy. Jambajimbira threw the magic bones and said, "Let there be nuts and chickens for Kalib and Ngabi."

Jambajimbira threw the bones once again and said, "Please return my village, and may the village of my two brothers disappear forever." Jambajimbira's village returned, and everyone danced with joy. The brothers' village had disappeared, and no one saw or even heard of those two brothers ever again.

# DOWN IN MY HEART

I've got that joy, joy, joy, joy,
Down in my heart,
Down in my heart,
Down in my heart!

I've got that joy, joy, joy, joy,
Down in my heart,
Down in my heart today!

I've got that love of Jesus
Down in my heart,
Down in my heart,
Down in my heart!

I've got that love of Jesus
Down in my heart,
Down in my heart today!

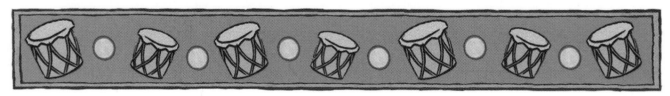

# THE DAUGHTER OF THE SUN AND THE MOON

Adapted by Nicole Blades
Illustrated by Rita Radney

**L**ong ago there lived a handsome young man who was the son of a chieftain. The young man's name was Kia-Tumba Ndala. All of the young women in the village watched Kia with smiles and bright eyes. He was the most adored bachelor around.

Soon the time came for Kia to choose a bride. However, he wanted only to marry the daughter of the Sun and the Moon, not a woman of the Earth as everyone expected. Kia's father, Kimanaueze, thought his son's wish to marry the daughter of the Sun and the Moon was silly.

"How will you get all the way up to heaven to propose to her?" asked Kimanaueze.

But Kia stuck with his wish, answering, "We'll see. But I'm not marrying anyone else."

As word spread about Kia's wish, the villagers began to think maybe he was under a strange spell. But Kia was so determined that he wrote a marriage proposal asking Lord Sun for his daughter's hand.

The problem was, how would he get it to heaven when he could not get up there himself? Kia went to Antelope and asked if she could deliver it, but she said it was too far. Kia asked Hawk and then Vulture, but despite both of them having wings, they turned Kia down. Hawk and Vulture said that they could only make it half of the way.

Frog overheard Kia's request and offered to take the letter to heaven. Kia could not see how Frog would be able to do it, but he gave him the letter anyway.

What Kia did not know was that Frog lived near the well from which Lord Sun and Lady Moon's helpers fetched water every day when they came down from heaven. Frog planned to stow away in their buckets and ride up to heaven and back without ever being noticed.

As planned, Frog made it to heaven hidden in a water bucket. When the time was right, he jumped out of the bucket, put Kia's letter on the kitchen table, and went back to hide. Soon Lord Sun came in for some water and saw the letter. He read it and was intrigued by the mysterious message.

Frog returned to Earth the same way he had left. He immediately went to tell Kia the good news.

"If you delivered it, then where is the reply?" Kia asked.

"I don't know," said Frog. "But I do know that Lord Sun read it. If you write another letter asking for an answer, I will again deliver it."

So Kia did. And Frog went back to heaven in the same way and left the letter on the table.

Lord Sun read Kia's letter and wrote back. Lord Sun said he would approve the marriage only if Kia came in person and brought a gift.

Kia was overjoyed when Frog returned with this reply. But the problem was again, how would Kia get to heaven?

Kia gave Frog a gift of gold coins to bring to Lord Sun, and Frog went to deliver the gift in his usual way. After Frog arrived, he waited until everyone was asleep, then tiptoed into the daughter's room.

Frog brought with him a magic needle and thread. He gently sewed the daughter's eyes shut. It was magical, so the daughter felt no pain.

When the daughter awoke and could not open her eyes, her worried parents sent messengers down to Earth to ask Doctor Ngombo for advice. Frog got back to Earth first by way of the helpers' bucket, and he raced over to the doctor's hut as fast as he could.

Luckily, the doctor had stepped away. So when Lord Sun and Lady Moon's messengers arrived, Frog hid behind the door and pretended to be the doctor.

Frog told the messengers to send the daughter to Earth for treatment at once. The messengers did as they were told.

When the daughter arrived, Frog snipped the magical thread away, and she could see perfectly! He then took her to Kia's hut. When they met, Kia and the daughter fell in love instantly. Frog, who did not like to be thanked, quickly hopped away. The lovers got married, and everyone was happy!

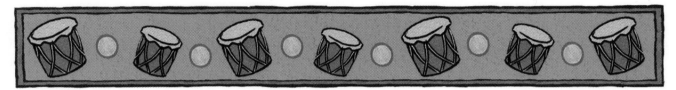

# GO TELL IT ON THE MOUNTAIN

Go tell it on the mountain,
Over the hills and everywhere.
Go tell it on the mountain,
That Jesus Christ is born.

The shepherds feared and trembled,
When lo! above the earth,
Rang out the angel chorus,
That hailed our Saviour's birth.

Go tell it on the mountain,
Over the hills and everywhere.
Go tell it on the mountain,
That Jesus Christ is born.

# Good Blanche, Bad Rose, and the Magic Eggs

Adapted by Eleanor Engram
Illustrated by Joey Hart

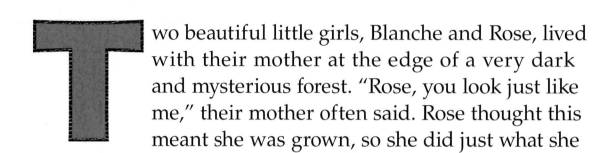

Two beautiful little girls, Blanche and Rose, lived with their mother at the edge of a very dark and mysterious forest. "Rose, you look just like me," their mother often said. Rose thought this meant she was grown, so she did just what she wanted and refused to help with the chores.

One day while their mother was sweeping the floor, she said, "Girls, we need some water. Please go out to the well and fill the bucket." Blanche jumped up, glad to go to the well, but Rose, pretending she did not hear her mother, sat rocking in her chair, playing with her bear.

Blanche went to the well and let her bucket down to get some water. Out of nowhere an old woman appeared. "Come here, little girl," she said, "and give me a drink of water." Blanche was a bit scared, but then she remembered that she always obeyed her elders, so she gave the old woman a drink of water.

"You are a good girl," the old woman said, and then she disappeared into thin air.

When Blanche went back to the well the next day, the old woman came again. "Follow me," the woman said. "You'll be safe."

Blanche followed the old woman deep into the forest. Startled by a noise, she turned, and right in front of her were two axe heads battling. "This is very strange," Blanche said, hurrying to get around them. Just then, out of nowhere, came two arms boxing each other. Blanche was afraid, but the old woman just laughed and said, "Come on, you are a good little girl!"

Just when Blanche thought she had all she could take, right in front of her, hanging in the middle of the air, were two witches riding on broomsticks. Blanche was terrified. She followed the old woman into the cabin and watched as the woman put a bone into a pot of water that was boiling inside the fireplace. The woman then put the pot on a table.

Blanche watched as the pot filled with a thick stew of meat, potatoes, and gravy. She turned in amazement to see the old woman and her chair begin to rise off the floor!

The old woman floated closer to Blanche. "Go in the back to the chicken house," she told Blanche, "and there you will find eggs that talk. Some will say, 'Take me.' Some will say, 'Don't take me.'"

The old woman continued, "If you do what they say, by the time you get home, you will have gold and diamonds and beautiful clothes."

Blanche did just what the eggs said. She filled her apron with eggs that said, "Take me," and sure enough, by the time she got home, her arms were filled with treasures.

Blanche's mother was very happy to learn about the old woman and the talking eggs. She turned to Rose. "Go," she said, "and bring back more riches than Blanche brought."

Rose hurried to the forest to look for the old woman. She passed the battling axes. She passed the boxing arms and then the flying witches. At last Rose came to the cabin, but she went straight to the chicken house. Some eggs were calling, "Take me!" and others were calling, "Don't take me!"

Rose did something very bad. Every time an egg said, "Don't take me," she grabbed it and put it in her apron. Rose said to herself, "If Blanche got all that by being good, I can get much more by being bad! I won't let those talking eggs fool me!"

Rose went back through the forest. The axes stopped fighting and chased after her. One of the boxing arms tried to grab her, and a flying witch just missed crashing into her. The eggs cracked open, and toads came out, crawling into her hair, into her pockets, and into the hem of her dress. Snakes crawled from other eggs and chased Rose back to her house. Her mother met her at the door. Snakes, toads, and all kinds of ugly creatures followed Rose into the house.

"Get out of here, Bad Rose," her mother cried as she chased Rose, the snakes, and the toads straight through the house and into the backyard.

Rose ran into their chicken house. "You will sleep there from now on, you disobedient child!" her mother cried. And Bad Rose really did spend every night in the chicken house.

# THIS TRAIN

This train is bound for glory,
This train.
This train is bound for glory,
This train.
This train is bound for glory,
Don't ride nothin' but the good and holy.
This train is bound for glory,
This train!

This train don't pull no extras,
This train.
This train don't pull no extras,
This train.
This train don't pull no extras,
Don't pull nothin' but the midnight special.
This train don't pull no extras,
This train!

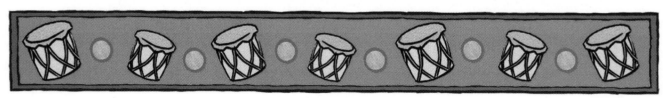

# TORTOISE, HARE, AND THE SWEET POTATOES

Adapted by Gale Greenlee
Illustrated by Angela Jarecki

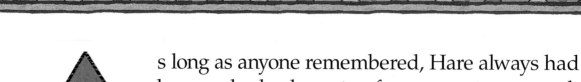

**A**s long as anyone remembered, Hare always had been a shady character, forever up to no good. He spent his days telling riddles no one could answer and playing pranks on the other animals in the forest. And each night Hare thought of new riddles and tricks he could play.

"I am the number one trickster," Hare said with a grin. "No one is more clever than I am."

Tortoise, unlike Hare, was a kindhearted creature. Each morning, she rose with the sun and happily began her daily chore of cleaning her teeny-weeny pond. She took pride in her housekeeping skills and kept the pond in tip-top shape, just in case a weary traveler ever needed a cool drink.

So Tortoise was not surprised when Hare dropped by one unusually hot autumn day. But being a friend of most forest creatures, Tortoise had heard of Hare's bad reputation. As Hare filled his cup with water, Tortoise thought, "Hare may be a swindler, but he won't fool me. I will never fall for his trickery."

All afternoon Hare tried his best to trick Tortoise. He told her his most difficult riddles, and she easily answered them. "This is harder than I imagined," Hare thought, so he tried something new.

"Miss Tortoise, please join me for lunch today," Hare asked sweetly.

"Mister Hare, we're nowhere near your home," Tortoise said, "and I have nothing in my cupboard."

"No problem," said Hare. "I know a field full of sweet potatoes ready for harvest. Let's go there."

Tortoise knew the field belonged to a mean old farmer. She did not care for the farmer, but she still thought stealing was wrong. She told Hare she would not go with him. But soon, her stomach began to grumble and growl. When Hare asked her again, she agreed, but with her own plan in mind.

Within minutes, they stepped into a giant sweet-potato patch. They pulled up sweet potatoes until their sack was full, then they built a fire and roasted the potatoes.

As Tortoise bit into a freshly roasted sweet potato, Hare said, "Hold on. What if the farmer catches us?"

Tortoise seemed unconcerned and continued to eat. She smacked her lips and said, "Oooh, this is good!"

"Shhh! Did you hear that?" said Hare. "We should check out the place and make sure it's safe!"

The two split up and went off in different directions. But Tortoise knew Hare was sneaky. When Hare was out of sight, she crawled into the sack to eat another potato in peace.

"Mmm, yummy!" Tortoise exclaimed. "I'll have just one more."

Before she could have another helping, sweet potatoes tumbled down all around her. It was Hare. He picked up the sack, flung it over his shoulder, and sprinted off hoping to leave Tortoise behind. "She'll never find me," he said.

"Boy, will Hare be surprised," Tortoise thought as she ate another sweet potato inside the sack.

After a while, Hare found a swimming hole. "Now I can drink some water, eat all the sweet potatoes, and not worry about Little Miss Slowpoke," he thought. Hare reached into the bag without looking, and Tortoise placed one of the last sweet potatoes in the hungry Hare's hand.

"Oh no," Hare thought. "Surely I can do better than this pitiful thing." Hare propped the bag up against a tree and put his hand back in, fishing around until he touched something big and warm.

"This will be a feast," Hare said. But much to his surprise, he did not pull out a sweet potato.

"Miss Tortoise!" he screamed as she rose from the sack, handing him the last pebble-sized sweet potato.

Then Tortoise grinned and said, "You may be a swindler, but you can't fool me. I'll never fall for your trickery."

Disappointed that his trick backfired, Hare cried and cried. As for Tortoise, she headed back to her pond, pleased with herself for fooling the forest's most famous trickster.

# Swing Low, Sweet Chariot

Swing low, sweet chariot,
Coming for to carry me home.
Swing low, sweet chariot,
Coming for to carry me home.

I looked over Jordan, and what did I see,
Coming for to carry me home?
A tall band of angels coming after me,
Coming for to carry me home.

If you get there before I do,
Coming for to carry me home.
Tell all my friends I'm coming too,
Coming for to carry me home.

I'm sometimes up, I'm sometimes down,
Coming for to carry me home.
But still my soul feels heavenly bound,
Coming for to carry me home.

# John Henry

Adapted by Vincent F.A. Golphin
Illustrated by Christopher B. Clarke

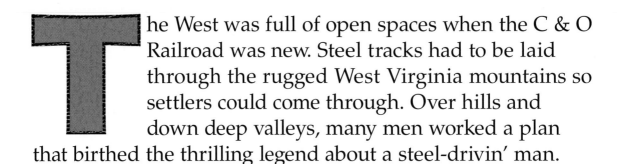

The West was full of open spaces when the C & O Railroad was new. Steel tracks had to be laid through the rugged West Virginia mountains so settlers could come through. Over hills and down deep valleys, many men worked a plan that birthed the thrilling legend about a steel-drivin' man.

"Keep on drivin'!" yelled the foreman. Mile after mile, the workers did race. For every section of rail set down, men hammered spikes to hold them in place.

One by one, workers lifted sledges and slammed the nails on the head. "Come on, keep up with John Henry," the foreman always said.

With skin as dark as midnight, shoulders wide as two trees, John Henry stood nearly seven feet tall. His voice carried a mile on the breeze.

He used a 30-pound hammer, nailing track faster than a four-man crew. The workers at Big Bend Mountain said he was the best they ever knew.

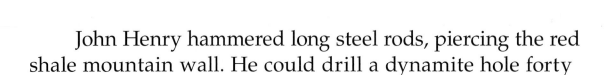

John Henry hammered long steel rods, piercing the red shale mountain wall. He could drill a dynamite hole forty feet when the foreman gave a call.

"Come over here, John Henry," the foreman said, "and make us another hole." The strong-armed giant drove that steel like he was digging for silver or gold.

The blaster lit the fuses, and the workers ran and hid. After the big explosion, they hauled rocks away on a skid. As a thousand men carved the mountain for $1.25 a day, the railroad owner told the foreman, "That's more men than we need to pay."

One day in 1870, the foreman told the workers about the C & O's plan. "We're going to use this steam engine drill," he said. "It's faster than a man. We've got to cut the Big Bend Tunnel, the biggest ever done. No man can drive these rods fast enough, not even a steel-drivin' one."

The angry workers shouted at the foreman. One after another asked him, "Why?" John Henry yelled, "Boss, a man never knows what he can do until he gives it a try."

"Bring the steam-powered drill closer," said the foreman to the engineer. The men let out a rousing cheer, and John Henry showed no fear.

The steam drill slammed one rod then another into that mountain face. John Henry's hammer answered each stroke to match the grueling pace.

Two or three hours soon passed, and people wondered how big John Henry would last.

The blaster set the charges after every rod was drawn. Explosions roared across the valleys as the race went on and on.

"Keep that steel a-comin'," John Henry said with a grin. The side of the mountain opened right up, and the steam drill moved on in.

John Henry drove those rods all day Monday, hammered away on Tuesday, too. When the rooster crowed on Wednesday, the race was finally through.

The steam drill cleared a mile-long path, slammed 130 rods. John Henry tunneled through a mile and a half, and won against all odds.

The workers all walked right down the shaft past the defeated iron drill. They marveled at what a man could do with the power of his will.

"He's a steel-drivin' man!" every worker yelled out. "Look, see what he has done!" Up on the other side of the mountain, John Henry smiled in the blazing sun.

The foreman told John Henry, "I'm sorry that I pushed such a plan. I should'a known that no engine could whip a steel-drivin' man."

"A man never knows just what he can do," a tired John Henry said. Then he heaved a long sigh and fell to the ground. John Henry now was dead.

He is buried beside Big Bend Mountain, right where the east-west tunnels cross. The spot has a statue and a plaque that tells of the hero who was lost.

# MALAIKA AND BR'ER RABBIT

Adapted by Gwendolyn Battle Lavert
Illustrated by Beverly Hawkins Hall

alaika cried when her mama went to the market to sell vegetables. Malaika hated minding the house and garden all alone, because then she had very little time to play. Mama told her, "You have to stay here and pick the peas from our garden."

As soon as Mama left, Malaika went to her swing to play for a few minutes. Br'er Rabbit, who heard what Mama told Malaika, popped up and said, "I can pick peas for you. Keep on playing, Malaika. Have fun!"

Malaika gave Br'er Rabbit a big basket and let him into the garden. When Malaika went back to her swing, Br'er Rabbit ate a whole row of sweet, tender peas in a minute. His full belly shook. His ears, tail, and big old feet wobbled.

Malaika came back after a while, let Br'er Rabbit out of the garden, and went back to swinging. When Mama came home from the market, Malaika was still swinging high and low. "Mama," she said. "A wonderful rabbit came by, and he picked the peas. I got to play all day!"

Malaika's mama took her over to the garden and showed her that Br'er Rabbit was not so wonderful. He had eaten all the peas. The basket was empty.

"If he comes back again," said Mama, "I want you to let him in and lock the gate. Your daddy will take care of Mister Br'er Rabbit."

The next day, Br'er Rabbit hopped on over to Malaika's house. "Hey, Malaika," he said. "This sure is a fine day to play in the sun. I will pick the peas for you. Go on and swing high and low."

Malaika stayed quiet, but she opened the gate for Br'er Rabbit. He hopped inside. White puffy tail, big old feet, flippity-flop he went.

Malaika locked the gate behind Br'er Rabbit. Up and down the sweet-pea row, ears just waving, Br'er Rabbit stayed all day. Then, really late, he dragged his full belly to the gate. It was almost time for Malaika's daddy to come home from work, too. But Br'er Rabbit didn't know a thing about it.

Br'er Rabbit called, "Malaika, let me out now! I am all finished picking peas."

Malaika stopped swinging and went to the garden gate. "Br'er Rabbit, can't you see that I'm playing? I love to swing high and low. Sometimes I almost touch the blue sky. I can't be bothered with you."

Malaika's daddy came home and saw what was in the garden. Br'er Rabbit, that's what — all ears, puffy tail, and big feet. "What are you doing?" asked Daddy.

Br'er Rabbit said, "Malaika let me in here, sir."

"I see what you're up to," said Daddy. "Now, I've got something better than pea pods for you."

Br'er Rabbit hopped to the gate, flippity-flop. Malaika and her daddy grabbed him by the ears and stuffed him in a gunnysack. They hung the sack in the wild honey-locust tree and left. Soon Mister Wolf came along. He heard Br'er Rabbit coughing in the gunnysack. "Is that you, Br'er Rabbit? What are you doing in there?"

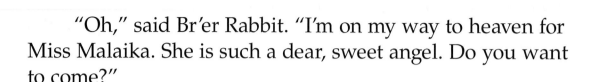

"Oh," said Br'er Rabbit. "I'm on my way to heaven for Miss Malaika. She is such a dear, sweet angel. Do you want to come?"

"Yes, indeed!" said Mister Wolf.

"Then open this gunnysack and come on in!" said Br'er Rabbit. So Mister Wolf jumped right in. Br'er Rabbit jumped right out and tied the wolf in the gunnysack. Br'er Rabbit was gone as fast as he could go. Malaika and her daddy came back and looked inside the sack.

"Mister Wolf," said Malaika, "what are you doing in there?" Malaika and her daddy laughed and let the wolf out. Then Malaika said, "When you see a gunnysack again, Mister Wolf, you'd better run as fast as you can."

Malaika added, "Make sure that Br'er Rabbit doesn't hide a trick in it, too!"

Now when Malaika goes to the market with her mama, she tells everybody, "I go around the bend. I see a fence to mend. On it is hung my story end."

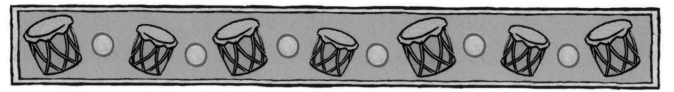

# When the Saints Go Marchin' In

Oh, when the saints go marchin' in,
Oh, when the saints go marchin' in,
Lord, I want to be in that number,
When the saints go marchin' in.

Oh, when they come on Judgment Day,
Oh, when they come on Judgment Day,
Lord, I want to be in that number,
When they come on Judgment Day.

When Gabriel blows that golden horn,
When Gabriel blows that golden horn,
Lord, I want to be in that number,
When he blows that golden horn.

When they go through them Pearly Gates,
When they go through them Pearly Gates,
Lord, I want to be in that number,
When they go through them Pearly Gates.

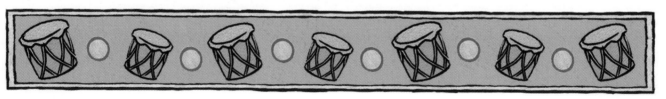

# WILEY AND THE HAIRY MAN

Adapted by Karima Amin
Illustrated by David Cooper

iley listened to his mama. She knew all about the Tombigbee River swamp and the terrible Hairy Man who lived there. Wiley's mama told him his papa had fallen into the river and was never seen again.

"If you go into the swamp, take your hound dogs," his mama warned. "The Hairy Man's scared of them."

One day, Wiley went into the swamp to cut some poles for the hen roost. While he was working, his dogs ran off after a wild pig. Wiley was alone when he saw the Hairy Man coming toward him, carrying a sack. He had bulging eyes and big, sharp, yellow teeth. Stiff hair covered most of his body, and his toes looked like cow hooves.

Wiley dropped his axe and climbed a tree. "Why are you up in that tree?" the Hairy Man asked.

"Mama told me to stay away from you," Wiley replied. "What do you have in that sack?"

"Nothing . . . yet," said the Hairy Man.

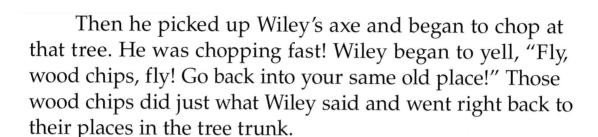

Then he picked up Wiley's axe and began to chop at that tree. He was chopping fast! Wiley began to yell, "Fly, wood chips, fly! Go back into your same old place!" Those wood chips did just what Wiley said and went right back to their places in the tree trunk.

The Hairy Man chopped faster. Then Wiley heard his dogs and hollered, "Here, dogs!" The Hairy Man tossed that axe and ran off through the swamp.

Back home, Wiley's mama said, "I know how to get rid of that Hairy Man. Next time you see him, say, 'Hello, Hairy Man. I hear you're the best conjure man around.'"

Wiley's mama continued, "A conjure man knows magic. Ask him to change himself into something big. Then ask him to change into something little. When he does, grab him and put him in his sack. Then throw it into the river."

The next time Wiley had to go into the swamp, he tied his dogs up at home. When Wiley saw that Hairy Man, he said, "Hello, Hairy Man."

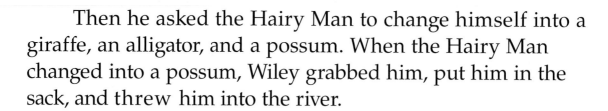

Then he asked the Hairy Man to change himself into a giraffe, an alligator, and a possum. When the Hairy Man changed into a possum, Wiley grabbed him, put him in the sack, and threw him into the river.

Then on the way home, Wiley saw . . . THE HAIRY MAN! Wiley climbed a tree — fast! "Hah! I changed myself into the wind and blew my way out of the sack," said the Hairy Man. "Come down here. I'm hungry!"

"Can you make things disappear, like the rope around my pants?" Wiley asked.

"I can make all the rope in the county DISAPPEAR!" growled the Hairy Man, and that is exactly what he did.

Wiley hollered, "Here, dogs!" The rope that held the dogs back home disappeared, and the dogs chased the Hairy Man away. When Wiley returned home, his mama said, "You tricked the Hairy Man twice. If we can do it one more time, we'll be rid of him forever." Wiley's mama sat down and closed her eyes to think. His mama could conjure magic, too!

For protection, Wiley crossed a broom and an axe over the window. Then he built a fire in the fireplace. His mama asked for a piglet from the pen. She put it in Wiley's bed under a quilt, and Wiley hid in the loft.

The dogs suddenly started to chase some wild animals, and then Wiley heard the Hairy Man on the roof. The hot chimney kept him outside, but at the front door the Hairy Man hollered, "Wiley's mama, if you don't give me your baby boy, I'll destroy everything you own!"

"I'll give the baby to you, if you promise never to come back," Wiley's mama offered. The Hairy Man promised, and Wiley's mama opened the door, pointing to Wiley's bed. The Hairy Man rushed in and discovered a piglet under the quilt. "This is a baby pig!" he roared.

Wiley's mama declared, "I never said which baby I'd give you." A very angry Hairy Man grabbed the piglet and ran off into the swamp. Wiley and his mama danced for joy!

And they never saw the Hairy Man again.

# THE COMING OF NIGHT

Adapted by Renée Deshommes
Illustrated by John Patterson

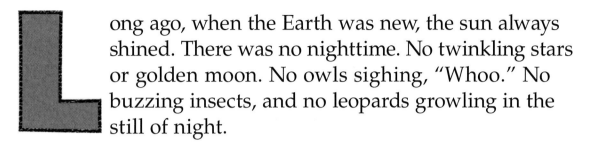

**L**ong ago, when the Earth was new, the sun always shined. There was no nighttime. No twinkling stars or golden moon. No owls sighing, "Whoo." No buzzing insects, and no leopards growling in the still of night.

The people did not know when to awaken because there was no dawn, and there was no dusk to tell them when to go to sleep. Sunlight filled the skies all the time.

Then one day Yemoya, the magical goddess of the river, sent her daughter Aje to wed Oduduwa, the Earth chief. Aje left her cool and shady home deep within the river and came to the surface.

Aje and Oduduwa soon were married. Aje loved her new home and husband, but as time passed she began to grow weary of the bright, hot sun. "Oh, how I miss the dark, cool waters of the river," Aje said. "Oh, how I wish Night would come!"

Oduduwa wanted his bride to be happy, so he asked, "What is Night? Where can we find it?"

"Night is a cool, crisp sheet that covers the day's warm bed," responded Aje. "It calms all who are weary, but Night can only be found beneath the water in my mother's home."

Aje and Oduduwa decided to summon Crocodile and Hippopotamus, the river's messengers. Aje wrote a note to her mother asking her to send Night to the surface. She gave the note to the messengers.

Crocodile and Hippopotamus swam deep beneath the water until finally they arrived at Yemoya's beautiful river palace. Yemoya read the note from Aje and began to fill a sack full of the mysterious Night for the messengers to bring back to Earth.

"Careful," Yemoya warned them. "Do not open the sack. Only Aje can control the night spirits."

Crocodile and Hippopotamus nodded, bowed, and then swam away with the sack. Once they reached the shore, they stopped to rest. Suddenly, a strange noise could be heard coming from the sack. It was the night spirits!

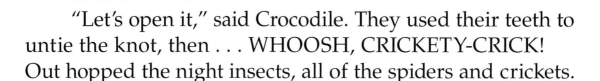

"Let's open it," said Crocodile. They used their teeth to untie the knot, then . . . WHOOSH, CRICKETY-CRICK! Out hopped the night insects, all of the spiders and crickets.

WHOOSH, WHOOO, CHIRP! Out flew the night birds, all of the owls and nightingales.

WHOOSH, GRRRRR, ROARRR! Out rushed the night animals, all of the lions and leopards. Night so terrified Hippopotamus and Crocodile that they jumped in the water and swam away.

Aje had been waiting nearby. When she heard the noises, she knew just what she had to do. She closed her eyes, raised her hands, and hummed a soothing lullaby. At once, the night spirits hushed, and all was peaceful across the land.

The insects scattered throughout the bush. The stars twinkled while the moonbeams glowed. The night birds nestled in the trees, and the night animals rested in the grass. A cool breeze blew in the night air. Aje had restored calm. Then she gave directions to balance Night and Day.

Aje smiled and soon fell fast asleep. Now that Night had arrived, Aje could at last be comfortable in her new home. Oduduwa was pleased that his wife was truly happy and had helped to bring the wonderful Night to Earth.

The people of Earth were happy with Night as well, and they welcomed the darkness, calm breezes, and mysterious sounds of the night creatures.

The next day, Aje decided to bring order to the land so there would always be a daytime and a nighttime.

Aje named the sun Morningstar and said, "Your job is to rise and begin the day."

She told the rooster, "You are the guardian of Night, and you shall crow to tell us when Morningstar is near." Aje also instructed the other birds to chirp sweetly at daybreak to help awaken all of the people.

And ever since then, the sun, rooster, and birds announce each new day, but only after the night has passed and all have had a restful sleep.